To My Family and the Future Generation.

For information about this title or to order other books and/ or electronic media, contact the publisher:

Dasengels Literary Ink™ 2019 at
dasengelscompany@gmail.com

Front Cover and Interior design by April L. Engels

Library of Congress Control Number: 2020904150

ISBN: 978-0-578-65643-4

First Paperback Edition, 2020

SOME TIMES
WE
FALL

BY
APRIL L. ENGELS

Table of Contents

Somebody's Journee

The rocks, broken glass, tumbleweed, and cactus stuck to her bloody and bruised knees as she crawled on the ground with the blistering palms of her hands. As she moved around and tried to look up, Journee didn't know where she was or how she got there. Her family and friends had warned her about driving through the forbidden desert alone. They told her to steer clear of it because people didn't always make it out alive. But here she was, all alone out in the open desert. She had to see so desperately what was out there.

In the distance, all she could see were cactuses, tumbleweed, and mountains. She knew she had been in the barren desert for hours and felt a dryness aching in her throat. Her lips began to quiver, and she tried licking them to relieve her thirst, but they still felt dry and cracked. While moving about on her knees, she began to grow tired and didn't have the energy to go on. She slowly came to a halt and fell over.

Thursday, August 16, 2018.

Journee sat at her computer smiling as she chatted away on Facebook. She was Darknlovey2018 and had met Hersheykisses4u two months ago. They had been chatting for a while and talked about their favorite foods, music, television shows, and what they liked to do for fun. Journee did most of the chatting and loved the attention. She always felt the world needed to know who she was and where she had been. On Facebook, Instagram, Twitter, and Snapchat, her life was an open diary for all to read. It was easy for anyone to know what she was doing and where she was going at any given moment.

***

After she felt comfortable enough with her long conversations with Hershey, the day had finally come for them to meet. Journee was so excited and admired herself while looking in the bathroom mirror. She continuously pouted, moisturized, and plumped her full lips with bright red lipstick. She loved how the color complimented her brown skin, hazel eyes, and short, brown, natural hair.

While looking down at her outfit, she tugged at the bottom of her red spaghetti strap tank, making her cleavage more revealing. She loved the way the top suited her skinny black jeans and was proud of her figure. Being 21 years old, she wanted to flaunt her looks and felt dressing a little sexy would help her catch that special someone she desperately sought. As she looked in the mirror once more, posing and taking many selfies, she noticed the time. "Oh, shit I better get going."

Journee sped off in her Toyota Rav4 and wanted to get to the ice cream shop before Hershey did. She thought she would scope him out before meeting him and hoped he looked like his Instagram pictures. In the photos, he appeared to be very tall, dark-skinned, had washboard abs, a chiseled jawline, and a gleaming white smile. To Journee, he was everything she always wanted in a man. She couldn't wait to touch, grip, and caress those bulging muscles. She felt he seemed too good to be true and often wondered why he was available. She thought any woman would have already snatched him up.

Making her way into the parking lot, Journee wondered about all kinds of things. She wondered if Hershey would find her attractive, intelligent, and kind. She also thought about what she would say and felt a little nervous. "Okay, this is just a date," she told herself. Once she parked, she looked at her face once more in the rearview mirror. "My makeup is on point," she giggled. Then, she adjusted her clothes and quickly hurried inside the ice cream shop.

"Hi, welcome to Stone Cold," the young, blonde-haired, woman said, eyeing Journee as she walked in. "Would you like to try a sample?"

"Yes. Mint chocolate chip please! And I'm also going to wait for a friend before I order anything."

"Ok," the girl gladly gave Journee a sample of ice cream.

"I'm Ashley by the way. Please let me know if you need anything."

"Okay, thanks." Journee sat down at a booth in the middle of the ice cream shop and rubbed her hands together as she anxiously stared out of the window. She wanted to know what kind of car Hershey drove or if he was going roll up on a motorcycle.

***

Thirty minutes had passed, and Journee kept checking her Instagram, Facebook, Snapchat, and Twitter accounts. She also posted status updates, took selfies, checked her email, and read the latest celebrity gossip. Then, noticing the time, she tried contacting Hershey on Instagram.

@Herysheykisses4u hey, where are u? I'm here. But he didn't respond. She watched customers come in and order her favorites from peanut butter cup to mint chocolate chip as she waited some more. She also enjoyed inhaling the fresh smell of baked cones that left a sweet and salty scent in the air. *Maybe he's already here.* She thought and started looking around. But he was nowhere to be found. Journee was furious and felt she waited long enough and angrily headed out the door.

Thursday, September 6, 2018.

Journee sat at her computer inputting contact information and worked as a receptionist fo*r Charter Times.* She had been with the company for two years. She was content with her job since it brought her one step closer to achieving her career goals. She was a senior and journalism major at Cal State Westridge University. Her goal was to become a successful journalist and report hard-hitting news.

As she typed away, her phone began to ding. Journee immediately pulled her phone out of her handbag and looked down at the screen. She couldn't believe her eyes. She had received an IM from Hershey. *Wow! Is he serious?* She thought as she read the message:

Hersheykisses4u: @darknlovely2018 hey. "I know this … ASSHOLE," she blurted. "Oh shit, let me be quiet," she whispered. *I know this boy isn't trying to talk to me after he stood me up! Boy Bye! What kind of fool does he think I am. He is acting like he didn't stand me up! I can't believe he has the audacity to try and talk to me. Like nothing ever happened. Like we're all good. No, honey. I can't. Boy, please!*

Journee was furious and turned her phone off with a look of disgust on her face. She couldn't understand why Hershey was trying to talk to her after all this time. To avoid thinking about him, she decided to bury herself in her work.

When her shift finally ended Journee shut down her computer, grabbed her purse, and went ahead to the elevator.

"See ya tomorrow, Ms. Anderson," the young black security guard said while pressing the elevator door open.

Journee gave him a friendly and sympathetic smile. She felt sorry for him and knew being a security guard seemed like the only job young black men get nowadays. This sometimes made her appreciate her career more. She knew it was decent and could've easily found herself working as a security guard.

Before pulling off in the parking lot, Journee turned her phone back on, connecting it to Bluetooth to play some music. Driving home from work and listening to Drake was the best part of her day. As she was beginning to bob her head to the beat, the music stopped. She looked at the radio screen and was trying to figure out what went wrong. The screen started flashing messages from Hershey. As they popped up, the messages played aloud in an auto monotone:

Hersheykisses4u: @darknlovely2018 sorry about not meeting you.

Hersheykisses4u: @darknlovely2018 I miss you.

Hersheykisses4u: @darknlovely2018 can we start over?

Hersheykisses4u: @darknlovely2018 talk to me, please!!!

Hersheykisses4u: @darknlovley2018 I'm sorry, I had a family emergency.

Hersheykisses4u: @darknlovely2018 I LOVE U!!! I WANNA BE YOUR MAN!!!

Hersheykisses4u: @darknlovely2018 are you there?

Hersheykisses4u: @darknlovely2018HELLOOOOOOOOO?

Hersheykisses4u: @darknlovely2018 Let's talk about this. I only have eyes for you.

Hersheykisses4u: @darknlovely2018@ Come on, baby, don't be like this!!!

Hersheykisses4u: @darknlovely2018@NOW I'M STARTING TO GET MAD!!!!

Hersheykisses4u: @darknlovely2018@ BITCH!!!!

Hersheykisses4u: @darnklovely2018@ I'm sorry, baby!!! I didn't mean to say that.

Hersheykisses4u: @darknlovely2018 Pleaseeeeee!!! Let me take you on a date and make up for it.

Hersheykisses4u: @darknlovely2018 YOU BETTER NOT BE TALKING TO SOMEONE...OR ELSE?????

Hersheykisses4u: @darknlovely2018 I'm sorry, baby. I didn't mean it. I was only playing.

Hersheykisses4u: @darknlovely2018 WHO THE HELL ARE YOU TALKING TO?...

"Wow, this dude is really crazy. Who is he calling a bitch? That mutha fucka don't know me. Ooh, he doesn't know me. Who the hell does he think he's playing with? Ooh, I CAN'T," she yelled. "I can't believe this shit! When I get home, I'm blocking his ass. This fool is crazy!"

When Journee eventually made it home, she kicked off her black high heels, unfastened the buttons on her blouse, and took off her black mini pencil skirt. Then, she proceeded to her tiny kitchen and reheated leftovers. While her food warmed up, she made her way towards the bedroom to finish getting undressed. Looking in her oak dresser drawer, she found her favorite cotton sweatpants and a loose-fitting gray t-shirt. She quickly put them on, grabbed her food, poured herself a glass of wine, and sat in her favorite black reclining chair in the living room.

She turned on the television, and *World News* with David Muir was on. She intently watched the tv as he explained how police officers killed another black man. *Wow, they shot him in the back while his 5-year-old daughter and wife watched in horror. The police are probably lying about him fitting the description of a burglary suspect and finding a gun.* Journee's heart sank as she thought about the story. She felt sorry for the family and shook her head in disgust. She wasn't surprised by the news. She knew the officers would probably get off. Then, there would be a community outrage, another Black Lives Matter march, with no results. Then, the news would follow up, claiming the young man was in a gang. These stories upset Journee. The media had a way of making people believe these stereotypes and assumed this was every black man's story, and this is why Journee wanted to become a journalist. She wanted to make a difference and report the truth.

After hearing too many horror stories, Journee decided to flip the channel to something more lighthearted. She loved watching reruns of *Martin, The Jefferson's,* and her quietly kept guiltiest pleasure, *The Golden Girls.* Her mother had introduced her to these tv classics. While laughing, eating, and sipping on her red wine, Journee looked at her purse sitting beside her and pulled out her phone. She turned it on, and instantly, she began receiving text messages non-stop from Hershey. She didn't bother to read them and decided to block and unfollow Hershey on all her social media accounts. After unfollowing him, she started getting new friends request right away. *This dude is a psycho! Okay, now he is beginning to scare me!*

Freaked out by Hershey's behavior, Journee thought about calling one of her friends or even her mother. But she contemplated for a minute and decided not to call anyone, especially her mom. She didn't want to give her the satisfaction of telling her, "I told you so." Journee knew her mom's predictable outcomes always came true. Her mother told her repeatedly that people can be whomever they wanted online. She warned her to steer clear of social media and quit telling her business to the world. Her mother's favorite saying was that "Something's we're better left unsaid." But Journee didn't care; she craved the attention. She kept on posting things about herself online almost every day.

***

At ten o'clock, Journee let her body hit the cool, crisp cotton sheets with ease and drifted off peacefully to sleep. It was several hours later when she was startled by a loud thumping noise. "Oh, shit what was that?" she said while peaking from underneath the covers. It sounded like someone was walking in the living room. So, she slowly pulled back the covers and grabbed a metal baseball bat that she kept underneath the bed. Then, she slowly tip-toed carefully and cautiously towards the bedroom doorway. When she made it to the end of the hallway, she peeped into the living room and saw no one. Feeling a little more confident, she edged up slowly, stretched her arm out, and flipped the light switch on in the living room. She looked around, and everything seemed to be intact. Feeling at ease, she decided to check the front door. "Why is this door unlocked? I remembered locking it last night. Or maybe I thought I did?" she murmured to herself.

Before heading back to bed, Journee peaked through the blinds in the living room and looked down in the parking garage. In the shadows, right behind her car, she thought she saw a person standing there. To make sure that she wasn't seeing things, Journee ran over to the light switch, turned on the porch light and looked out the window again but didn't see anyone.

***

The sun began to peer through the bedroom window, and Journee could feel its warmth touching her face. She slowly opened her eyes to embrace the sun. As the rays beamed across her face, she thought about the noise she heard and wondered if she dreamt it. Looking at the clock on the wall, she immediately got up to get ready for work.

Journee let water finish dripping down her back as she stood in the shower allowing herself to air dry. The fresh rosy scent of Dove stung and burned her nostrils as she looked down at her long feet. She wanted to stay in the shower a few moments more and cringed at the thought of the cool air hitting her body when she got out. She slowly pushed the door open and grabbed her pink cotton towel hanging on the nearby rack. When she finished drying off, she moisturized her skin with Palmers' cocoa butter, sprayed a light scent of *Poppy Coach* in the air, and felt it prickle all over her body.

By the time she finished getting ready, it was going on 8 o'clock, and Journee found herself searching for her car keys. She usually hung them on the keyring in the kitchen whenever she returned from somewhere. She started looking underneath the cushions of her sofa and once more in the kitchen. *Where are my damn keys? I'm going to be late. Forget it! I have to go.* She was running out of time and needed to be on the road by 8:15. So, Journee grabbed her spare key, headed for the front door, and was a little hesitant as she stepped outside. She remembered the apartment keys; we're also on the misplaced keyring.

Before leaving, she decided to look under the black rubber doormat outside her apartment. She ran her hand underneath it but couldn't feel a key. So, she lifted the entire mat and saw that it was gone. *My Mom must have taken the keys. She always forgets to put it back.* Then, she remembered she was able to lock the door from the inside.

Journee drove off and started to wonder about everything. *Damn, I'm starting to forget things and shit, scaring myself a night. That fool Hershey has me tripping. Ooh, I'm done with him*! She turned on the radio to put her mind at ease. She drove highway 138 every day to beat the early morning traffic on the freeway. It was one of the most dangerous highways to drive. Multiple deadly accidents had always occurred on this road. But Journee felt she was a good enough driver and had no doubts of getting into an accident. She had been driving 138 for the past two years and figured since nothing has ever happened, she'd be all right.

Journee slowed down and saw the light turning yellow up ahead. When she made it to the intersection, she turned her music down to make sure she didn't hear any fire engines or an ambulance coming. As she waited at the light, she looked in her rearview mirror. *What's that in the back? I could've sworn I saw something moving around.* The light turned green, and Journee slowly made her way across the intersection. She looked in her rearview mirror once more. "AHH ... ," she screamed loudly. She was startled and horrified by a hunched over tall white man with a rugged beard, skinny tight eyes, and short buzzed cut, who had scratches all over his face. He slowly appeared from the back-cargo space. Journee continued screaming, taking her hands off the steering wheel as the car veered aimlessly off the side of the road.

"Keep your hands on the damn wheel," the skinny, thin, beaded-eye man growled while making his way over the backseat.

Journee's heart was pounding so fast and felt as though it was going to burst out of her chest. While she panicked with fear, she struggled with her seat belt. Instead of unbuckling it, she managed to restrain herself to the seat very tightly. The car continuously rolled aimlessly further into the desert while it accelerated. Journee's foot had become heavy on the gas pedal as she became frozen with fear. Her legs felt like they had bulky weights attached to them. She frantically tried to control the wheel and saw what was left of a burned-down brick house out in the distance ahead. The car was heading straight for it, and the scrawny, rough-looking man fell forward, smacking his head against the passenger seat. Journee screamed even louder. The man grabbed her by the arm, and she tried to pull away from his hold. She let go of the wheel and punched him in the face. "You little Bitch!" he grunted right before the car collided with the wall.

There was nothing but complete darkness, broken glass, and the sound of a horn continuously blaring out in the open. Dust and steam seeped and silhouetted around the crushed and mangled front end of the car into the air. Journee arms lay lifelessly at her sides while her head laid nestled in a billowy white, ballooned cloud. The warm sensation of blood rolling down her face began to agitate her. She awoke from the darkness and couldn't remember what happened. Her head was throbbing from impact. As she looked around, everything seemed so surreal. As she sat back and looked up, she saw the car had collided with what was left of a brick wall. She noticed the front windshield had been shattered and looked as though someone had gone through it. "Oh, my God," she cried and remembered the skinny white man. She began trembling and shaking with fear and looked behind her. The man was gone. She started fumbling with her seat belt and managed to unbuckle it.

Journee also tried several times to push the driver-side door open, but it wouldn't budge. So, she pushed with all her might, and it finally gave way. She immediately fell to her knees in the dirt and didn't have the strength to lift herself. She moved about looking for the man, but he appeared to be nowhere in sight. She kept on crawling until she was on the opposite side of the brick wall. To her surprise, she saw the scrawny white man. His eyes were wide open, and he was looking in her direction with his face covered in blood from ejecting through the front windshield. He was in a slumped-over position that seemed unreal. His neck appeared broken, and one side of his face laid rested in the dirt along with shards of glass. His face looked as though it was resting on a pillow. At the same time, the lower half of his body was in a doggy-style position. Journee could also see that his pants had been stripped off of him. She saw the man's bloody, bruised, and mangled ass sticking up in the air. *He's dead!* She thought and sighed with relief. She rolled onto her back and closed her eyes.

***

The sun began to set, and a cool breeze of wind blew through the open desert and grazed Journee's face. The sensation caused her body to stir and quiver. She fought to open her heavy eyelids and managed to open them slightly. She could see the sun setting in the distance and had slept for hours. She rolled over on all fours and began crawling back to the car. She tried looking for her phone to call for help but couldn't find it. Her body ached all over with intense pain. She began to grow tired, and her eyes closed once more.

The night had come and went. Journee woke up to the familiar childhood chalky, dry taste of dirt in her mouth. She could feel the warm sun shining above her. She looked up and slowly rose her bruised and bloodied hand into the air. She was trying to figure out what time it was and remembered seeing something like this on the discovery channel. From the rise of her hand, she could tell that it was around noon. As she looked up into the air, she saw something tiny flying over her. The object was shaped like a square and looked like a toy plane hovering around her. It appeared to be a drone, and she pulled herself up and sat up on her knees. With little strength she had left, she began waving her arms in a state of distress. The drone started to lower itself down, and Journee began to cry. She knew help was coming soon.

***

Her Mother sat at her bedside, watching her sleep. Journee's eyeballs were racing, making her eyelids flutter. Her Mother stood up, leaned over, and kissed her on the forehead. She hoped Journee would be waking up soon.

The repetitious unconscious state of Rapid Eye Movement (REM SLEEP):

The rocks, broken glass, tumbleweed, and cactus stuck to her bloody and bruised knees as she crawled on the ground with the blistering palms of her hands. As she tried to look up, Journee didn't know where she was or how she had got there. Her family and friends had all warned her about driving through the forbidden desert. They told her to stir clear of it because many people didn't always make it out alive. But here she was, all alone and wanted to see so desperately what was out there.

As she tried to open her eyes and look around, all she saw was the open desert, cactus, tumbleweed, and mountains in the distance. Her lips began to quiver, and she tried to lick them to quench her thirst, but her lips still felt dry and cracked. Soon she began to feel tired and didn't have the energy to go on. Laying there on the ground, she realized all her bad decisions had finally caught up with her. She knew she should've listened to her mom, family, and friends. She remembered her mother always telling her that "It's better to not go looking for things. Sometimes you may end up with something you don't want," but Journee was stubborn and hard-headed. She was the type of person who always wanted to prove everyone wrong. Even after all the horror stories she heard, Journee still did the exact opposite.

Oh, I don't want to die like this. Please, God! She cried. *I just want to live.*

The Awakening

Journee slowly opened her eyes and felt the rays of sunshine beaming down on her face from a window. She slowly looked around and found herself surrounded by four white walls with a few posters on them. They offered advice on life-saving techniques, exercising, nutritional information about a well-balanced diet, and diabetes. Echoing in her ears were the sounds of monitors beeping and chirping. Looking down at her right arm, she saw an IV attached to it. Then, near her bedside, she also saw a familiar black leather jacket draped across a pale pink hospital chair. She knew it was her mother's jacket and anxiously tried to sit up but felt too weak.

As she began to move around in her bed, a young, white nurse with short blonde hair and brown eyes appeared in the doorway. "Great, you're finally awake. Don't try and move. I will lift your bed so you can sit up a little more comfortably," she says walking over and placing her foot on the handle at the left side of the bed." The bed slowly lifted

Journee in what seemed like a sitting position. "I'm Nurse Willie," she added and gave Journee a sympathetic smile.

Journee seemed a little confused and wanted to ask so many questions.

"I know you must have a lot of questions?" the Nurse expressed while checking her vitals and writing them down. She told Journee how she was at Clearview Medical Hospital and had been in a car accident three weeks ago and was placed in a medically induced coma. "Your parents are also here and went to grab a bite to eat in the cafeteria," she said while shining a flashlight in Journee's eyes.

"Well...who? Or how did I get here?" Journee says weakly in a thin, raspy voice.

"Let me pour you some water."

"You were discovered by highway patrol who were routinely scouting the area from a drone. Now, I'm not a huge fan of drones," the nurse continued, "but in matters of life and death. I'm thankful."

"There was a man..." Journee says, trembling.

"He didn't make it," the nurse retorted abruptly. "You should get some rest. I'll get your parents. They will be happy to know you're awake. Now is there anything else I can get you before I go?"

"The man…he…he…" Journee said softly with a worried look on her face."

"Sweetie, he's gone. You're okay and have nothing to worry about," she said sympathetically. "I'm going to alert the doctor and get your parents," and the nurse hurried out the door.

***

Journee was released after spending a few more weeks in the hospital. She had gone home with her parents until she was able to regain her strength. While recovering, she learned all about her attacker. The man in her backseat was Charles Lee Ray. He had been released from prison and was out on parole. The police told Journee that he had been stalking her for weeks and befriended her online as Hersheykisses4u. He had also followed her home from the ice cream shop. It was the day she was supposed to meet him. The police had also found her car keys in the man's jean pockets.

Journee was frightened by all this information. The police had also warned her about the dangers of social media and to be careful about posting things online. They mentioned how people are easily preyed upon just by what they post. They suggested she kept her friends list short and narrowed it down to family and friends she knew personally.

After almost losing her life, Journee decided to live a much quieter life, especially one that didn't involve the internet. She vowed to stay away from social media and stop desperately looking for love. She no longer sought out the attention of others and felt her life should remain private. What she now desired the most was dignity and self-love.

Beautiful ugly

Television, billboards, magazines, and celebrities all taught her to be beautiful in this world; you had to look a certain way. Tall, thin, fair-skinned, full lips and wear clothes that were revealing. Somehow in this make-believe world, Dawn thought this was reality. This idea of looking beautiful hypnotized her. She really wanted to be those women she saw on television and in magazines. She admired their frivolous materialistic lifestyles and tried her best to live by their standards.

Paydays would give her every opportunity to live out that fantasy. As soon as Dawn's check was deposited into her checking account, she would go straight to the mall and spend every cent on clothes, shoes, and makeup. She didn't care about saving money because her parents gave her everything she needed.

Although, having plenty of material things isn't what Dawn desired the most. What she really wanted was her parents' love and attention. Over time, their love was replaced by giving her things. To Dawn, the more they gave her, the less she felt loved. Her parents made her feel as if she were a distraction. They were always trying to get her out of their faces.

At the earlier age of twelve, Dawn started to notice her parents seemed less interested in her. As she grew into her adolescent phase, she had many questions about life, and her parents ignored them. The older she became, the happier they seemed to become. At times while growing up, Dawn felt as though she was raising herself. Most of her life lessons came from what she saw on television and observed in the real world. Being an only child, she often longed for an older sibling.

* * *

Dawn walked through the front door, slamming it loudly. "Mom, I'm hooommmeee," she emphasized. She was willing to do anything to get her mother to acknowledge her. She knew slamming the door was a definite attention-getter. Knowing this would upset her mom, was very amusing to Dawn. For her, any type of attention was better than getting no attention at all. Before making her way upstairs, Dawn peered in the living room to see if she saw anyone. To her surprise, her mom was sitting on the couch.

"Goddammit, Dawn, I told you several times to stop slamming that damn door."

"I'm sorry."

"No, you're not. You do that shit every time!"

"The door slammed because of the wind."

"Dawn, do I look like a fool to you?"

"No," She quickly retorted with a sly smirk upon her face. She could see her mother looking down at her shopping bags.

"So, I see you're still spending all of your money."

"Yep! And I earned every cent."

"Girl, one day you're going to wish, you saved your money."

Dawn shockingly laughed at her mom. "You shouldn't be the one to talk. All the money you and Dad spend on trips and eating out."

"Watch your mouth girl. We take our money and spend all of it on your skinny ass. You know what Dawn? Why am I even explaining myself to you? Girls stay out of grown folks' business."

"I am grown," Dawn murmured underneath her breath and headed upstairs. She threw her bags on the bed and sat at the foot of it. She took off her stiletto heels, caressed, and rubbed the bottom of her feet. Then, she dumped all her shopping bags out and carefully hung up a red fishnet dress and a red matching bra and thong set. She folded the rest of her clothes and put them in a dresser drawer.

After putting her things away, Dawn smiled and thought about how good she would look for the evening. *I'm going to be looking hella cute at the club tonight. The guys are going to be like: "Damn baby," and the girls are going to be like: "No, this chick didn't," Ooh, I can't wait. I'm going to be killin' em.*

***

It was around 9 o'clock when Dawn woke up. She had dozed off while lying in bed. She quickly got up, took a shower, and started getting ready for the evening. She smiled as she put on her new matching bra and thong set with the skintight, fishnet dress. She loved the way everything looked on her. The dress tightly hugged the curves of her hips and stopped right below her butt. The push-up bra also made her breast appear much bigger. "Yas, girl. Ooh I'm going to be pulling them tonight. Hi, I'm Dawn," she said while admiring herself in the mirror. She slowly started spinning around and continued talking to herself. "I know right. Of course, you can buy me a drink... No stop it...You stop it," she giggled.

After playing around in the mirror, Dawn sat down at her vanity table, oiled her cornrows, and put on her waist length wig. Then, applied repeated layers of foundation, pink eyeshadow, and a shimmering ruby red lipstick. Looking in the mirror, she was satisfied with the finishing touches.

***

When Dawn arrived at "The Palace" nightclub, bar, and lounge, she parked her car in the valet. She felt as good as she looked and wanted to make a stunning entrance. She knew everybody would be looking at her if she paid for prestige service. To her, it meant she was somebody.

As she got out, the young parking attendant didn't know what to do with his eyes. His face turned a slight shade of red, and he tried to avoid looking at her as much as possible. He tried to focus on looking down at the ground.

Dawn quickly took notice and giggled. "Don't be shy boo, it's okay to look."

He coyly smirked and kept looking down to avoid making eye contact.

She handed him the keys to her Mercedes. "Don't scratch my baby."

Then, she switched, swiveled, and slowly walked past him in her four-inch stiletto heels. She casually looked back to see if the young man was staring at her, but he didn't. She frowned a little. *I know I look good!*

As she stood in the long line waiting to get into the nightclub, she noticed people were staring at her outfit. She saw their coiled eyes and frowns. She stared right back at them with an attitude. She thought about how jealous they seemed. *Hmmm…don't hate, cause yo' man want me. Girl, please! You wish you could look this good.* While she was greeting their stares, a heavy-set, black man dressed in a black suit pulled Dawn out of line. "Hey beautiful you can go ahead," he uttered and nodded towards the other bouncer waiting at the door.

As Dawn made her way through the entrance, everyone looked her way, the D.J. on the turntables, bartenders, waiters, people sitting in the V.I.P. section, and everyone on the dance floor. Dawn smiled and felt like Cinderella making her grand entrance at the royal ball. She walked over to the bar and felt her phone vibrating in her clutch. She quickly took it out and read a text message from her friend Nicole:

Hey, girl, where are u? I'm in line waiting outside.

Dawn texted back:

I'm already inside; I got V.I.P. boo. I will come get u.

Nicole replied:

Whaaat??? How u managed that? Hey, I brought someone with me.

Dawn: I'm coming out now.

Dawn showed the bouncer at the door her wristband and told him that she had some friends waiting in line. She pointed out Nicole with a young, medium build, black guy. "That's them," she pointed and smiled. "Hey, girl." Dawn heard the snickers, laughter, and nasty comments once more. She and Nicole's eyes met. Her friend immediately stepped in front of her date, like a mother would protect her child.

"Heyyyyy girrrl" she stressed, looking Dawn up and down with shock.

"Damn, Nicole what do you have on? You look like a preschool teacher. No wonder why you can't get in."

Nicole was still looking at Dawn. She couldn't find the right words to express her feelings. She couldn't believe Dawn was wearing underwear with a fish net.

Dawn just smiled at her with curious eyes. "I know right," she said, slowly spending around.

The bouncer was still waiting for them. "You ladies coming in or not?"

"Yes."

"No."

"Girl, what are you talking about? Let's go. He'll get in; she said, smiling at her date. "I'm Dawn, by the way."

"Hi, I'm Derek," he said, looking her straight in the eyes. "Move it," the bouncer uttered rudely.

"You know what Dawn; I'm going to stay with him. We'll see you inside."

"Girl, are you sure? I got this."

"Yes," Nicole said quickly.

"Alright, girl. You're trippin." Suit yourself. See ya' inside." Dawn walked back into the club and felt as though Nicole was acting funny. She didn't know why she was tripping. Dressing provocative was her and Nicole's usual thing back in the day. She also couldn't get that ridiculous image of Nicole dressed like a schoolteacher out of her mind. The more she thought about it, she began to realize that Nicole had changed since going off to college.

***

Dawn looked at her phone and noticed twenty minutes had gone by. Nicole and Derek still weren't inside. She sat her martini down on the table and headed outside. She looked down the line and didn't see Nicole or Derek. All she could see was envious eyes staring back at her and the constant echoes of "hoes, and skanks," as she looked on.

"That's why Ya'll asses are still out here," Dawn told the crowd. Many responses immediately met her comments.

"Say, that shit to me when I get inside."

"Skank."

"How much you charge?"

"What corner are you working tonight?"

"Her flat ass blacker than the Deep South."

"Is that your tit's or raisins?"

"You better learn how to walk in them heels."

"She got her wig at the Halloween store."

"My back fat got a bigger cup size than that."

"My two pieces from Popeyes has a bigger breast than that."

"Girl bye, with that cheap ass underwear set on from Ross."

The insults continued, and Dawn tried to ignore them, but they started to bother her. Everyone in line even started laughing at her. As she angrily walked back into the club, she threw both her middle fingers in the air. She was giving everyone in line the bird. She went back to her table and couldn't understand why Nicole would leave.

Where the hell is Nicole? I know her ass didn't leave me. Dawn started to get angrier by the minute and thought about calling and texting Nicole. When she did, she got no response. She didn't know why Nicole was tripping. *Maybe she thought I was going to take her man. I do look hella good. Well since I'm already here, I guess I might as well enjoy myself.*

***

Dawn ordered several drinks and danced the night away. All kinds of men approached her. She would dance with them, and they told her all sorts of things about marriage, babies, and sex. Dawn laughed at their comments and enjoyed every moment of it. She was also surprised that no one picked a fight with her. Deep down inside, she knew they wouldn't because they would be thrown out.

Around 3 o'clock in the morning, Dawn started feeling extremely tired and began to stumble on the dance floor. She had danced and drank for hours and knew she would have to call a cab to get home. She stopped dancing and looked around, and everything seemed as if it were spinning. Suddenly, she started to feel queasy, feverish, and sick to her stomach.

"Damn, baby you, okay?" The tall, black guy said trying to hold her up. "You got to stand up, they're going to kick us out. AYE," he yelled again as she leaned on his shoulder. Dawn didn't respond. Everything started to appear blurry to her. She began to pass out, but before she could. She saw the bouncer who let her in earlier walking towards them in the crowd. She slowly closed her eyes and collapsed on the dance floor.

***

Her nose twitched from the sour smell of piss in the air, and it caused her to nearly gag. She felt her head throbbing and slowly began to open her eyes. As she looked up, she could see the morning sky as clear as day and quivered from the cool breeze in the air. She looked around, and to the right of her, she saw a big green dumpster. She began to breathe harder, and her chest heaved in and out rapidly. She stumbled on the pile of dirty cardboard boxes that were beneath her. She looked down and noticed her clothes were gone. Her mouth dropped open, and she could barely make out a sound. It was like someone had knocked the wind out of her after being punched in the gut. When the air finally made its way through her lungs, Dawn let out a loud deafening scream.

The High Life

He was a well-rounded, young, respected individual in the black community. Everyone admired and adored Jackson. He was like everybody's son or brother. The younger kids looked up to him, while the adults knew he would do great things. For Jackson, this meant anything other than playing sports. He felt in the black community; some people believed this was all one could do. But deep in his heart, he knew he could be anything. He wanted to be the next doctor, lawyer, astronaut, or even an engineer.

Jackson smiled as he walked home from school, admiring his report card. He made straight A's for the fourth time in a row and knew his parents would be proud. He thought about how they would celebrate by going to dinner and where he'd like to eat. *Let's see. The Olive Garden? Nah, too much pasta makes my stomach hurt. Plus, I'll get full off the salad and breadsticks. Maybe we should go to the Outback. Nah, it's always packed, and we'd have to wait a while for a table. Let's see... The Cheesecake Factory Nah...the cheesecake is the only thing I would want to eat! Prime Lobster? Nope they like to microwave their seafood. Man, I'll just let Mom and Dad choose.*

Jackson was halfway down the block when he felt his phone vibrating in his pocket. He took it out and saw a text message from his friend Craig.

What's up, Jack? Come over and game.

Let me guess, Fortnite?

Yep.

Ok, Craig, let me ask my parents.

I know u about 2 Lie.

Yep, u know they don't want me hanging out with ur crazy ass.

Jackson called his mother and told her about his grades. She was ecstatic and suggested going out to dinner like he thought she would.

"Jackson, I am so proud of you!"

"Thanks, mom... Hey, I was calling to let you know that I'm staying after school to work on a project."

"Okay, baby. Well, don't be late for dinner."

"Okay, I will be home by six. Thanks, Mom." Jackson hung up quickly before his mom began to ask more questions. Then, he texted Craig back:

Hey, omw fool.

Alright, Jack. Grab some Doritos from Gino's Liquor Store.

K, see ya soon, C.

When Jackson got to Craig's house, he could smell the foul stench of weed in the air. Walking up the steps, he contemplated whether to go in or not. As Jackson grabbed the door handle, he could hear Craig laughing and yelling. He walked in and immediately started choking from the smoke lingering in the air. He could see Craig sitting on the floor in front of the television with a joint in his mouth.

"Hey, what's up action Jackson?" Craig said, looking back at him. "Why your parents gave you a last name for a first name?" he giggled.

"Why your parents named you Craig? That shit is ghetto as hell."

"Oh, you got Jokes?"

"You're a Joke. I told you not to invite me over when you're smoking that shit. Your gonna' have my parents tripping. I'mma be pissing in cups again."

Craig began to laugh even more.

"Why you gotta say 'smokin that' shit?' Man, you act like I'm smoking crack. This shit is strictly for medicinal purposes. So, just chill with the D.A.R. E and drug free program."

"First of all, Cannabis is a gateway drug."

"Cannabis! Ha...ha... ha... You're stupid," Craig grunted while laughing louder as he took another puff of his joint. "Who the hell says: 'Cannabis?' What are you a scientist?"

"Fool, it's weed, grass, ganja, broccoli, Mary J and my personal favorite 'the shit,' he giggled. "Oh, yes, it is! You sure you don't want to hit this?"

"Nah, man, quit playing around. Get that shit out of my face. Like I said, "that shit is a gateway drug?"

"No, it's not. Scientifically, it hasn't been proven."

"Ok, maybe it hasn't, but it's still been known to increase your chances of experimenting with other drugs."

"Damn, Jackson why you gotta' kill my high? Chill. This shit is harmless. Do you see my ass acting a fool?"

"YES! Your ass is already acting goofy and shit. Eating and sleeping all damn day. Your slow as hell and can't even think straight," Jackson quickly pulled the Doritos from his backpack. "Why Craig?... I mean I just don't get it."

"I told your ass, it's for medicinal purposes."

"Please, your Pops is the only one that's in pain. If he finds out what you've been doing, man yo' ass would be grass."

"Yes! My ass sure does like this grass," he laughed. "Damn, Jackson why you trippin? I'm good. This shit is good and relaxing. My Pops don't know shit because this house smells like weed all the damn time. Plus, my homie always hooks me up with a refill anyway."

"Whatever fool. Your ass is already addicted, that's why you keep smoking it. You better be careful buying shit off the street. I'm telling you; people can lace that shit with anything."

"Man, ain't nobody trying to hear that shit, Jack?"

"Dispensaries are the best way to go, it's clean and it's regulated."

Craig started laughing loudly, "You sound like a goddamn commercial. Yo' ass is funny. Man, ain't nobody regulating shit."

"I'm just saying that's how most people get hooked on drugs. When your dope man wants to increase his profits, he surely will hook your ass up with something stronger."

"Damn, what are you, my sponsor? Or do you want to game? Plus yo' ass is already getting high off contact. Them eyes getting red. You sure you don't want to hit this?"

"Man, get the shit out of my face."

***

Jackson and Craig gamed for hours. It was already after seven when Jackson looked down at his cell phone and noticed several missed calls from his mother.

"Damn, man I'm late."

"What? You pregnant?"

"Shut up!" Jackson laughed as he got up.

"Nah, man, I'm supposed to be going to dinner with my parents. "I gotta go."

"Alright, man. Congratulations on making the honor roll. Just so you know, your mom's is going to beat the shit out of you."

"Whatever, bye Craig!"

As soon as Jackson got home, his parents could smell the foul stench of weed on him. "Ouch! What's that for?" His mother smacked the back of his neck.

"I told your ass to stop hanging out with Craig."

"Mom, I…"

"Boy, shut up. I don't want to hear anything you have to say. You're not going to be satisfied until that boy gets you hooked on them drugs. How come you lied to me?"

"Mom, I…"

"Boy, shut up!" His dad came over and got in his face and stood close enough to kiss him. He pressed his forehead against his and looked Jackson directly in the eyes. "Boy, are you smoking dope?"

"No, dad…I"

"Did I tell you to speak?"

"No...sir."

"Give me your damn phone. You're grounded and I don't want to hear a damn peep out of you. No phone, music, or television. The only thing you're allowed to do under this roof is eat, piss, shit, and sleep. From now on we're picking your ass up, to and from school. So, you might as well get comfortable and disassociate yourself with that weed head. It's going to be a long month," his dad emphasized.

"Yes sir."

"Now get the hell out of my face." Jackson jumped. He was frightened by the rows of wrinkles forming across his dad's forehead. He could feel the bass in his dad's voice trembling with anger. To him, he sounded like the black man in those Allstate commercials.

***

Jackson spent the next four weeks staring at Kevin Durant, Michael Jordan, and James Harden posters on his room walls. Every day when he'd come home from school, he did chores, ate dinner, did homework, showered, and laid in his bed reading books. He had begun studying for the college entrance exams and wanted to review everything he learned throughout the year. He was looking forward to getting into a prestigious university.

While being stuck in the house, every day when his parents got home from work, they would ask him about school and continuously gave him lectures on drugs. His Mom and Dad would even take turns. They told him how today's youth has become destroyed by drugs, especially in the black community. They talked about how others wanted to see him fail because he was young, black, and intelligent. His parents also explained how fortunate it was to go to school, given the nature of black history.

"Son, with knowledge comes power," his dad said, resonating his voice. "And if college isn't for you, then you need to do something with your life. Don't sit around here, smoking dope, and waiting for something to fall out of the sky. If you do nothing, you get nothing. It's up to you to be somebody. Don't be a nobody. You understand me son?"

"Yes, sir."

Jackson had to listen to this speech every day. He had heard it so much that he could recite it word for word. He knew his parents kept repeating this speech because they wanted to protect him from the harsh realities of the world.

Eventually, when Jackson got his freedom back, he did stir clear of Craig for the most part. His parents made sure of it; by picking him up from school and showing up at his hang out spots. They also continuously made him pee in cups over the next couple of weeks and checked his phone for messages from Craig.

But behind his parent's backs, Jackson still tried to keep in touch with Craig. He used the alias Brenda for Craig as a phone contact. Every now and then, he would get a text message from Craig. Most of the time, he didn't hear from him at all. Eventually, it got to the point where Jackson couldn't keep up with Craig, and their relationship drifted apart.

***

Graduation day had finally arrived, and Jackson stood proud in his black cap and gown. He stood 5 ft 9, dark-skinned, clean- shaven, with a nicely trimmed haircut. He leaned into the microphone and could see his parents, aunts, uncles, and cousins standing in the bleachers. They smiled, cried, and hugged one another.

They were so proud of him. He was the only black male student in his class to graduate valedictorian. Not only was his family and friends proud, but every black face in the crowd felt extremely proud too. Jackson even got a little teary-eyed as he looked out into the crowd. He felt the presents of what this moment meant to the black community and all people of color. Then, he spoke:

"Thank you, mom and dad, for pushing me as hard as you did. Thank you for keeping me in check. You have steered me clear from all the dangers out here in the world. You have kept me safe and, most importantly, protected me from myself and those who did not want to see me make it. And here I stand.

To my classmates, do not let anyone or anything stop you from pursuing your goals and dreams. It is a long and rocky road, but it is up to you to avoid the danger along the way. So, always try to follow the clear path ahead of you. I know there are times when we may feel like our parents, guardians, or even some of our friends may tell us about ourselves, and we may not like what they have to say, but sometimes it is best to listen. We have our entire lives ahead of us, and believe me, you do not want to waste it. Sometimes we rise, and sometimes we fall. So, listen to that tiny voice inside your head. The one that is telling you to do the right thing. This way, you will not be easily misled in the wrong direction. Thank you."

Jackson stood back and watched the crowd come to their feet. They let out a roaring and thunderous applause. He felt victorious and enjoyed the admiration.

***

Jackson and his dad sat at the kitchen table, looking over all his college acceptance letters. "I can't believe my son is going to college. Dartmouth, Howard, Stanford, USC, and UCLA. Which one are you going to go to son?"

"I don't know Dad. Which everyone is the farthest?"

"Watch your mouth?" His Mom laughed while flipping a pancake. "Why don't you take the trash out?"

"Alright, Mom."

Jackson pushed the backscreen` door open and made his way down the wooden steps. He looked around and could see his neighbor Jesse through the gate in his backyard. After dumping the trash, Jackson made his way over to the side gate. He could hear and see Jessie breathing hard as he was lifting weights. Jessie took notice of Jackson and slowly sat the weights down.

"Hey, what's up Jessie?"

"Sup Man. Congratulations on graduating."

"Thank you."

"So, you heard about Craig?"

"No, I haven't heard from him in months. What's up with that fool anyways? He was supposed to graduate this semester?"

"Dude, got caught up."

"Caught up! How?"

"His pops found out about his extracurricular activities and kicked him out. This happened a couple of months ago. I saw that idiot on Tenth and Western Avenue begging for money."

"What? Are you serious?"

"Yeah, man. He kept on hanging out with all those low lives. I told him to stop hanging out with them before he ended up just like em.' I guess he apart of the click now."

"Damn, I can't believe that shit."

"Yeah, it's a damn shame."

"Wow. All right well I'll catch you later."

As Jackson made his way back into the house, he thought about all kinds of things. *I should check on that fool. See if he's okay. He couldn't have fallen off like that.*

"Jackson are you okay? Did you see something? You look worried."

"Mom, I'm fine... Just thinking."

"Thinking about what?"

"What school I should go to."

"Well, don't think too hard," She laughed. "I'm quite sure all those schools would be lucky to have you."

But Jackson was really concerned about Craig. Later, that day he told his parents he was going to the park to play basketball. Although, he really headed to Tenth and Western Avenue.

He quickly made his way to the west side of town, where everything looked abandoned, worn down, and littered with trash. As he continued towards Tenth and Western, Jackson contemplated what he would say to Craig and wondered if he'd even recognized him.

When he got to the corner, he saw an old rundown apartment building that looked like it was from the

50s. Surrounding the building, he could also see what appeared to be a homeless encampment. There were tents, grocery baskets filled with random objects, trash, and broken glass all over the ground. Jackson anxiously stood on the corner, looking out in the open to see if he would get a glimpse of Craig. As he waited impatiently, a black, 1976 Supreme Cutlass pulled up next to him. Jesse looked in and saw a young black man smoking a cigarette.

"Hey boss what do you need?"

Jackson froze and didn't know what to say. He looked in the car and couldn't believe his eyes. He saw Craig fidgeting in the back seat.

"CRAIG!" Jackson shouted.

"You know this fool?" the young black man, said looking back.

"Uh, yeah. Let me talk to him for a minute," Craig quickly replied.

"Alright, but we need to talk about what you owe me," the man said, gripping a pipe from underneath his seat.

Jackson was frightened and wanted to leave. He thought about telling Craig he'd talk to him later.

He watched the man behind the steering wheel get out of the car. Jackson noticed the gun tucked in the man's waistband. The man eyed Craig and padded the gun as he let him out of the backseat. Jackson stood frozen and didn't know what to say or do. He knew he shouldn't have come, but he just wanted to check on Craig, and now he was having doubts about the whole thing.

"He...man...what's up?" Craig said, reaching out with his right hand and clasps his in Jackson's, giving him a partial hug.

"Congratulations on graduating and shit. So, what are you doing on this side of town?"

"I came to check on you."

Craig laughed at Jackson. He looked Jackson up and down while rubbing his chin.

"I'm good, man. So, let's talk for a minute. Loan me fifty dollars. So, I can get this fool out of my face. Then, we can catch up on old times."

Jackson didn't hesitate and pulled his wallet out of his back pocket and gave Craig fifty dollars. He thought he was being a good friend by giving him the money. He didn't mind and just wanted to talk to Craig. He thought maybe he could get inside his head and convince him to do the right thing.

"I'll be right back."

Jackson watched Craig get back in the car, and the man pulled off. He looked on, watching the black cutlass making its way over to the rundown apartment building. Craig got out of the car and looked back at him. He gave Jackson a wave of assurance, letting him know he was coming back.

Thirty minutes had gone by, and Jackson decided to leave. When he eventually made it to the next block, Jackson saw numerous black and white police squad cars and DEA vans flying right past him. He knew exactly where they were going, Tenth and Western Avenue.

As he continued walking back to the nicer side of town, he felt bad for Craig. *I just can't believe that fool. Well, at least he'll get the help he needs while being locked up. Jeez, I almost got caught up. Damn! I could be getting arrested right now. Never again! Mom and Dad were right!*

***

Jackson looked out his bedroom window and could see flowers beginning to blossom, new leaves sprouting on the trees, and butterflies hovering in the air. *Yep, spring is officially here!* He thought while grabbing the last of things out of his dresser drawer.

"You ready?" his dad called from downstairs.

"Yes." Jackson took one final look at his room and the photo frame that sat on his dresser. It was a photo of him and Craig when they were twelve. He shook his head with a heavy heart. Two days after the drug bust on Tenth and Western, he learned that Craig had overdosed. Knowing Craig had died tore Jackson apart on the inside. He felt guilty about giving Craig money that day. He thought then maybe he'd be alive.

Jackson's parents tried to explain to him that it wasn't his fault. They told him Craig chose that life. Even if he wanted to help Craig, it still wouldn't be left up to him. They told Jackson that sometimes you can do all you could to help people, but they must be willing to help themselves. Jackson tried to keep this advice in mind, but the thought of seeing Craig going into that building seemed to haunt him forever.

The Ultimate Shopping Experience

Sara

Sara casually walks into ShopCo and grabs a shopping cart. She is dressed in an extremely loose-fitting, oversized, black sweatsuit in the middle of summer. She is also carrying an enormous handbag that is empty and heads straight over to electronics. She politely smiles at the sales floor associates and watches them as they restock inventory and tend to other customers. She casually makes her way over to electronics to look at all the latest DVD's and music CD's. Then, she looks around for security cameras and eyes them while slightly turning her back. Since no one is paying attention to her, she easily slips CD's and DVD'S into her handbag. Then, she heads to the main entrance to leave the store.

Layla

Layla had just got off work and wanted to surprise her son with a reward for making the honor roll. Before making her way into the store, she looked at her reflection in the glass sliding doors and admired her outfit. She was dressed in one-inch black heels, a gray blazer, with a matching knee-length skirt, while her hair was neatly pulled up in a bun. She also wore a natural light makeup that accentuated her high cheekbones and dark complexion. She smiled at the sales floor associates and the white security guard standing at the door. She loved shopping at Shopco as opposed to other stores. At Shopco, it was easier to get the things she needed without the hassle of extremely long lines. While walking throughout the store, she had one main goal: to get her son's favorite movie. As she made her way to the electronics section, a young white woman walked right past her. *It's too damn hot for that shit! She's making me hot with that sweatsuit on!*

As she browsed the DVD section, she could hear the camera above her head zooming in on her. *Now that shit is pissing me off.* Layla looked up, smiled, twirled around, and waved at the camera. The other shoppers looked at her with puzzled looks on their faces, and the sales floor associates looked on with bewilderment. Layla found *Black Panther* in the Marvel superhero section and quickly grabbed it.

"Excuse me miss. Can I help you with something?" A young Asian man said approaching her.

"No, you cannot," she said with an annoyed look on her face. Earlier, two associates had asked her the same thing.

"Well, if you need help," he said, raising his eyes brows. "Please let me know."

"Mmm—hmmm," she quickly retorted.

"I can check you out right here, if you'd like?" he persisted while gesturing to grab the DVD.

"No, thank you. I'm not done shopping yet. Can you please go bother somebody else?" The young man angrily walked away towards the checkout and picked up the phone.

As Layla continued browsing the DVD section to see what else was on sale, she heard an announcer over the P.A. system. "Security please scan and record the electronics section." *Now I'm pissed off! I'm going to buy this movie from somewhere else. This is a damn shame!* She thought and started heading for the exit.

Sara

Sara took her hoodie off as she made her way to the glass sliding doors. The young white security guard smiled at her as she made her way through the exit. The electronic security system beeped, and she giggled, "My goodness! It must be my car keys."

"It's ok Ma'am. You're ok," The security guard said, waving casually and gesturing for her to go ahead. "Have a nice day!"

"Thanks, You too!" *Wow, that was too easy. What a dummy!*

Harold

He continued to smile at the young beautiful blond woman as she smiled back at him. Harold loved his job and felt he was great at it. He also proudly carried a flashlight, twist ties and wore a uniform that made him feel important. As he was admiring his uniform, he heard someone talking over the radio.

"Harold. You copy?"

"This is Harold," he said, putting the radio extremely close to his mouth.

"We have a possible shoplifter heading for the main exit. It's a black female, 5 foot 4, wearing a gray skirt suit, one-inch black heels and carrying a small, wallet size, handbag. Stop her."

"Copy that."

Layla

Layla was furious and thought about speaking with the store manager but didn't waste her time. *They always think folks are about to steal, especially, black people. They need to check their employees. Their asses are the ones stealing. I bet they didn't even approach or say anything to that young white woman wearing winter clothes in the middle of summer.*

"Excuse me miss."

"What?"

"Ma'am, you're going to have to come with me."

Layla looked at the young white security guard like he was crazy. She widens her eyes, and rolls of wrinkles formed across her forehead. She looked at him confusingly and couldn't understand why he was stopping her.

"For what?"

Harold grabbed her by the arm.

Layla tried to pull her arm a loose. "Boy, if you don't let go of my arm..."

He reached for his radio down at his side as he struggled to keep a tight grip on Layla. "I need backup."

"Let go of me!" she protested. Everyone that was standing around started staring at them. They immediately pulled out their cell phones and started recording.

He wrestled her to the ground and put his knee in her back.

"You're hurting me. I can't breathe."

Harold ignored her pleas, and there were four other lost prevention team members headed his way. When they arrived, three of them helped Harold to pin Layla to the ground. At the same time, the fourth member pulled out plastic handcuffs and put them around Layla's wrist. When he finished, they all got off her and tried lifting her off the ground. But Layla didn't move. She laid motionless as the four- team members continuously told her to get up. So, Harold turned her over and saw blood coming from the corners of her mouth. He began panicking and pacing back and forth saying, "OH. MY.GOD!" as he cried.

The customers screamed at the employees, "YOU KILLED HER!" While somebody yelled, "CALL 911," as the rest of the customers looked on in horror.

<u>Kevin</u>

Kevin called her cell phone repeatedly, but he was not able to reach her. The last time he heard from his wife was around 7 o'clock, and it was going on 8 pm. He began to worry as he and his son prepared dinner. "Charles see if you can reach your mother one more time."

Charles called his mother, and her phone went straight to voicemail.

"Dad, she didn't answer."

"Ok, try your grandparents house," he said, turning the television up to hear the 8 o'clock news.

"Hey Dad, isn't that the ShopCo by our house?"

Kevin turned the volume up on the television and saw a reporter standing in front of the store, and the headline read: "Suspect Killed While Shoplifting." Then, footage obtained from a shopper showed a woman being wrestled to the floor for several minutes and then laying motionlessly on the floor.

Charles dropped the phone in horror with tears streaming down his face. His father fell to his knees in horror and let out a gut-wrenching cry.

Two weeks later, all four ShopCo employees and the security guard were arrested. They were charged for manslaughter and were only sentenced to two years in prison. The police pulled the video footage from the store and proved Layla hadn't taken anything, but the footage also revealed a white woman stealing several things. She was eventually identified and arrested.

After learning this information, the black community was outraged and protested in Layla's honor. They marched in front of ShopCo, chanting how she was a victim of a hate crime and racial profiling. The community showed so much support for Layla's family that it even sparked a nationwide boycott at all ShopCo shopping centers. The store sales and stocks plummeted drastically, causing all the stores to eventually close.

Layla's husband and son grieved for months over her death. They sued ShopCo and were paid millions. But no amount of money could replace the pain Kevin and his son felt in their hearts.

I remember the first day we met. I was sitting on a bench in Central Park, taking in the view after a nice two-mile jog. Eminem was blasting in my earbuds, and I was bobbing my head to the beat. Then, as I got up without paying attention, I dropped my phone. When I was about to pick it up, a dark-skinned, firm-looking, masculine hand grabbed it. And as I slowly stood up, our eyes met. He had soft brown eyes and a gleaming white smile as wide as the sea. He was gorgeous, sophisticated-looking, and stood about 6 foot 2. I was mesmerized by his handsome face and charming smile.

"Hey, thanks!"

"No problem," he said, flexing his muscles in his shirt. Oh, he looked delicious! I just wanted to touch his bulging arm muscles. They seemed so firm, hard, and were perfectly sculpted.

"Eminem, *Lose Yourself*?" he uttered curiously.

I laughed. "Yes, I love that song because it really gets you going."

"Is that right?"

"Yes!"

"I don't know about that old school fool. I'm more of a breathing in the air type a guy. I just love listening to nature and enjoying the scenery."

Bullshit. "Well, okay I can respect that."

"I'm Mark by the way."

"I'm Lisa." Our hands locked for a moment, and I couldn't stop smiling.

"So, you jog here often?"

"Most days when I'm not working. What about you?"

"I'm usually here on the weekends. Some days I usually go to the gym after work."

Okay. Brotha has a job! "So, what do you do?" I just had to ask desperately.

"I'm a Dentist."

Well, damn! Hello and thank you, God!

"What about yourself?"

"I'm a Marketing Director at Vivid Ads. We aim to please." Ok, I can't believe I just said that!

"Oh, wow! So, you're responsible for all those crazy ads I've seen on T.V?"

"Crazy! I highly doubt that," I laughed. "Our commercials are funny, uplifting, and entertaining."

"Sorry, I didn't mean to offend you."

"Non taken. You're only being honest."

"So, you mine if I join you?"

Hello! Brotha' could join me anywhere. "Sure, I'm on my last run."

Five months, two weeks, and three days later, we ended up living together. Our days were routine. We'd wake up early, make love, shower, eat breakfast, and part ways. On weekends we would go for our jogs in Central Park, to dinner, and sometimes on a quick romantic getaway. Everything in our world seemed so perfect. We were infatuated with one another.

Then one day, I told Mark I was taking a girl's trip to Vegas. So, I could catch up with my friends. For the past five months, I had been wrapped up with Mark. I felt it was time to get some breathing room and reconnect with my girls.

"So, babe is that cool?" he didn't respond. "It's only for a week and I think we need to give each other some space.

Maybe you can catch up with your friends." Mark stared blankly into the vanity mirror and kept on brushing his teeth. I stood in the bathroom doorway, patiently waiting for an answer. He arched his eyebrows and looked at me with a frown on his face. Then, he rinsed his mouth out. "Hello?" He hesitated and looked at me with a cocky smile.

"Yeah, babe it's cool."

He didn't seem so happy about it.

"Well, like I said it's only for a week. I really want to catch up with my girls. Spend a little time relaxing, shopping and talking with my girls. Is that okay with you?"

"I SAID IT'S FINE!" he yelled and stormed out of the bathroom.

Wow! His response caught me off guard. I quickly turned around and shouted at him, "WHO THE HELL ARE YOU YELLING AT?" He didn't answer and started getting dressed extremely fast. "Mark, don't you hear me talking to you?" He was buttoning his white collared shirt. This fool was still acting like he didn't hear me. So, I almost knocked him over, grabbed my black heels and purse. I didn't have time for this shit. "Ok, so your ass wants to start acting dumb. We'll

I'm going on my trip? I don't need your permission anyway. I'll see your stupid ass later."

***

The week of my trip had finally arrived. Mark moped for days. He acted as if somebody close to him had died. I didn't know why he was acting this way. We spent every day together. Hell, we live together! Even when we're at work, we will text each other, meet up for lunch, and call each other on our commute home. Some may even say this was highly toxic. Hell, even obsessive!

I remember going to visit my mom just two days before the trip. She was shocked that Mark wasn't going with me.

"Vegas, that sounds nice baby. So, is Mark going? That man never skips a beat. He's always right beside you. It's like he's your shadow."

"No, mom. He isn't going."

She looked at me with wide eyes. "What? How did you manage that? He acts like he can't live without you?"

"You really think Mark act's that way?"

"Yes." She said with no hesitation. "I can't even talk to you on the phone without him in the background trying to get your attention. You don't come over often because he takes up most of your time. We hardly get a minute alone."

I laughed.

"Your funny. Mark just loves me that's all."

"Yeah, like a drug. I'm telling you, that man is cuckoo."

"Dang, mom, I'm not about to go there with you."

"You shouldn't let him move in. You don't know anything about him."

"Mom, please! I'm about to leave," I quickly retorted, grabbing my car keys off the countertop.

"Damn, Lisa why are you leaving so soon? I was about to make us some lunch."

"Mom, I have to go."

"Let me guess, Mark? So, you don't have time to each lunch with your Mama?"

"I will mom. I promise. When I get back from my trip."

"No, you're not."

"Bye, mom." I politely kissed her on the cheek, and she just frowned with her tiny beaded brown eyes.

"Bye, baby."

***

I was so excited the day I went on my trip and met my girls at the airport. We had been friends for years and met in college. There was Candance, my go-to girl for everything. She was very outspoken, petit, and beautiful, but don't get on her bad side. Although she was small, Candance seemed to stand tall while in a confrontational mode. Then, there was my girl, Lauren. She was incredibly wise beyond her years with beautiful light brown eyes, a winning smile and was quick to call you out on your bullshit. She was like a Mama bear, always watching over us and keeping us in line. Then, there was the adventurous, intelligent, and witty Justine. She always made us laugh and got everyone to step out of their comfort zones. She was tall, stunning, confident, and always determined to get what she wanted in life. Justine always took pride in her looks when it came to everything. She always had to be on point, even if she was going to the grocery store. I loved my girls. We were close and felt more like sisters than friends. We seemed to have an unbreakable bond and had been through everything together. We were always there for one another.

As I stood waiting in the check-in line, I saw Justine pulling four suitcases (all Louis Vuitton, of course!) along with a matching carry-on. I immediately waved at her, and she hurried over towards me. "Damn, girl we're only going to be there for a week! Are you trying to relocate?"

She started laughing.

"You know me girl; I always have to come prepared."

"Yeah, you do. So, are you ready to have some fun? I can't wait to get a deep tissue massage, chill poolside, shop, and go dancing."

"Yes, I'm ready. The question is: Are you ready? I already know your ass is going to be on the phone with Mark the entire time."

"Jeez, Justine."

"Jeez, my ass! Girl, every time we go out, you're always on the phone with him. That shit always kills our vibe. It's like yall eat, sleep, and breathe one another. Girl, that shit isn't normal."

"Girl, Mark is my baby boo. I think it's cute how he checks in on me."

"Okay, if you think being stalked is cute! Go ahead with your bad self."

I frowned.

"Justine, please don't start, ok? This trip is our chance to let our hair down and have some fun. I don't need a lecture on relationships. Please!"

"Alright, but…"

I interrupted her before she could say another word. "Justine?"

"Okay," she said, rolling her eyes.

"Oh, there's Candance and Lauren." We both waved at the same time, and they came running over. We all hugged like we hadn't seen each other in years.

"Hey girls," Candance beamed with a smile from ear to ear. She was excited because this was a much-needed trip. She had been working on overload as a district manager for Macy's. She stayed in meetings, driving back and forth while being a wife and mother. "I can't wait to cut loose and relax for the next couple of days. No work, driving, husband, or kids. Yass!"

While huddled in a circle hugging one another, I felt my phone vibrating in my pocket. I immediately knew who it was and thought about responding but didn't want to catch heat from my girls. So, I just looked at my screen.

"Jeez girl, you can't even wait."

"Chill, Candance. You don't even know who this is?"

Then, they said all in unison:

"Mark!"

I laughed and had one missed call and several text messages from him. "Okay, yall right! I promise it's going to be all about us on this mini getaway. I will not be answering my phone. Starting…" I hesitated, "Now." I quickly turned my phone off and put it in my pocket.

"Yes, girl." Justine budded in. "We can't have Mark ass interrupting our trip. His ass is always calling every time we hang out."

"You don't need to turn the shit on, until after the trip."

"Okay, Justine. I'm not."

"If you do, I'm putting your phone in the trash."

"Okay and your ass will be buying me a new phone."

We all started laughing and made our way through the metal detectors towards our gate. We chatted while waiting to board the plane. Everyone talked about what we were going to do first, and we all couldn't wait to see Kendrick Lamar in concert.

***

The plane descended, and we were very anxious to get off. Inside McCarran International Airport, it was buzzing with thousands of travelers and nearly took us an hour to get our luggage and make it out of the airport. With all the busy commotion and loud noise, we couldn't wait to get out of there.

We stayed in a suite at the Nobu hotel. We loved our suite; it was luxurious, spacious, and had adjoining rooms. The girls and I claimed our rooms and beds. Then, Candance, Justine, and I started looking at the view of the pool from the surrounding windows. I just wanted to dive right in. "Hey, let's go chill poolside and unwind. I can't wait to expose this full-figure and these toned legs."

"Girl, now you know…"

"Damn, Candance please don't get started. I'm not about to call, or text Mark."

"Yes, because we don't have time for that shit. You need to leave your phone in the room."

"Girl,   please!"

"Please, my ass!"

"Ok, chill you guys," Lauren said, laughing as she came out of the bathroom. "Anyways, how do I look?" She had quickly put on her swimsuit while the rest of us had been mesmerized by the pool.

"Good," we all said in unison.

"Candance and Lisa let's try not to talk about Mark anymore. We're here to have fun. So, let's…do …this…girls," Lauren said, clapping her hands between every word. We all started laughing and pulling out our bathing suits and sandals.

I started getting dressed and thought about taking their advice. I knew they were right. Mark always ruined my time together with my girls. This time I was going to leave my phone turned off. So, I made a promise to myself that I was going to put Mark aside and live life for the moment.

***

We all enjoyed ourselves at the pool and spa that afternoon. We got mud facials, deep tissue massages and were pounding Cadillac margaritas. We chatted and met a lot of people. Everything was going well, and the atmosphere was just right. The sunshine beamed on our backs while lounging by the pool. We laughed and caught up on old times, took turns dipping in and out of the pool, and did a little innocent flirting with the youngins.' They were trying to impress us, and Candance, with her young-looking ass, seemed to be pulling them left and right. She entertained the young men with her girlish charm and got us a few rounds of free drinks.

As the evening drew on and the sun began to dip into the horizon, we ended the evening chilling in the Jacuzzi. "Oh, I so needed this," I said, taking the last sip of my margarita. Everything felt so relaxing.

"Yes, you did girl. You really needed a break from Mark."

"Damn, Candance here we go again."

"All I'm saying is that you need some space."

"I know that shit is so toxic. What's up with him anyways?" Lauren added. She just had to ask. She tossed her long cornrows over her shoulders and widened her brown eyes at me. "Well…?"

I stood up and sat on the edge of the Jacuzzi's top step. The bubbles and steam started to make me feel a little nauseous. They were all looking at me and waiting for an answer. "Damn, you guys, I thought we wasn't going to talk about Mark. We're supposed to be on vacation."

"Look, Lisa we're just concerned. It's just that… Mark seems to be very high strung."

"I know Candance. You guys don't have to keep reminding me. Mark and I are just infatuated with one another. I agree. We do spend a lot of time together."

"Too much time, if you let me tell it," Candance retorted.

"Well, I just think Mark has some attachment issues. His parents disappeared on him when he was 12 years old. They left him playing in the park and never returned. He spent most of his life in the foster care system and was never adopted out. So, yes he is a little high strung in that sense."

"Damn, girl I'm sorry that happened to him, but I really do think he has to address those unresolved issues," Lauren replied with extreme concern. "I'm telling you Lisa, that is a red flag. I've watched enough of Investigation Discoveries and…"

"Okay, Lauren I'm going to stop you right there. For one, Mark has always respected me in ways you can't possibly imagine. I already know what you're about to say. Mark is not about to go psycho on me because he has a slight …"

"SLIGHT!" They all said simultaneously.

I looked at them like they were crazy. I was becoming furious by the minute and wanted to cuss them out. They already knew the golden rule when it came to giving relationship advice. You can't tell a woman about her man and vice versa. So, why were they testing me?

"Ok, everyone just chill. I am starting to get pissed off. Let's just enjoy the rest of our trip. I really don't want to talk about Mark anymore. Okay?" Everyone went quiet. Candance, Lauren, and Justine all looked at one another. They were silently communicating like they wanted to say more.

"You're right Lisa. We're sorry."

"Speak for yourself Lauren," Candance mumbled. Her short ass always had to get the last word.

"Ok, let's get out of here and get dinner. Then, let's do *Thunder from Down Under*," Justine screamed while shaking her hips in the water. We all laughed, knowing her ass was about to make a fool of herself at the show. We knew Justine was going to try to make it on stage. She was thrilled about seeing a bunch of men dancing in tight- fitted jeans and exposed rock-hard abs.

Day two. We all slept in and had a thrilling night at the show, and Justine was able to meet the men backstage. Then, we went dancing till 4 a.m. and made it back to the room around 4:45 a.m. That's when the room phone calls began. We were all too tired to answer.

It was around 2 p.m. when I woke up from a knock at the door. I thought, *"Who the hell could this be?"* I slowly got up and grabbed my robe. Candance was snoring in the bed beside mine, and Justine and Lauren were still asleep as well. So, I decided to close the adjoining room door quietly. Then, I pressed my face against the suite door and looked through the peephole. I blinked for a minute and couldn't believe my eyes. My heart was pounding, and I turned around quickly with my back against the door. It was Mark! At first, I thought I was dreaming, or I was still drunk from last night. Then, he began knocking again, and I opened the door quietly.

"Hey baby, Surprise!"

"Mark, what the hell are you doing here?" I whispered angrily.

"Damn, baby what's wrong? I came to see you. I was able to take some days off and wanted to surprise you."

"Well, I'm fucking surprise! This is supposed to be my girl's trip."

"Dang boo, you're tripping and..." he said, surprisingly.

I stepped out of the room quietly and into the hallway.

"Shh...you're going to wake the girls."

"Well, aren't you going to let me in?" he whispered.

"Hold on," I said, going back into the room and pushing him away from the door. As I made my way into the room, Candance was sitting up in bed.

"Girl, please tell me that isn't Mark?" she said, folding her arms. "Lisa, please tell me that isn't Mark?" She persisted.

"Girl, it is!"

"Oh, hell nah…that's the psycho shit we've been telling you about. Girl, I just can't…" She got out of bed and opened the adjoining bedroom door and woke up Justine and Lauren.

"Yall, aren't going to believe the shit," she said, disturbing them from their sleep. They sat up, looking dazed, and confused as I went out the door.

"Are you serious?" They all said simultaneously and loud enough for me to hear them in the hallway.

"Baby."

"Shut up!" I said, grabbing Mark by the arm and dragging him down the hall towards the elevators.

"Baby, you're hurting my arm. That's quite a grip… Damn, Lisa!"

I couldn't say anything and pushed the elevator buttons repeatedly until the doors opened. Then, I pushed his ass in and stepped in behind him. My hands were tightly clenched, and I started pacing back and forth. "Mark, why are you here? This is beyond nuts! I wanted to punch Mark in the face. "This is ridiculous! Well?"

"Baby, I was worried about you? I tried calling and texting you several times. I even called the hotel room. I just felt like something was wrong."

"Damn, Mark this is ridiculous! It's only been a day. You didn't even give me a chance to call. You need to take your ass back home. Right now! This is beyond crazy! My mind is blown. Damn, am I still drunk? What is going on with you? My ass must be dreaming! What the hell are you doing here?"

I didn't let Mark get a word in as we made it down to the lobby. When the elevator doors opened, I pushed his ass out along with his luggage and told him Goodbye.

"Lisa...wait...I...don't have a place to stay," was the last thing I heard as the doors closed.

When I made it back to the room, the girls were up. I could hear them talking shit through the door. I walked in furious, and they were all laid across the beds in their pajamas. "Lisa, that shit is psycho and beyond crazy," they all said.

"Girl, that is a big ass red fucking flag," Lauren added.

"Girl, what are you going to do with him?" Justine asked.

"I'm telling you that shit is stocker status," Candance protested.

"I know. You guys just let me figure this out."

"I would be done with his ass," Lauren replied.

"I would too," Candance and Justine both agreed.

"That shit is fucking nuts."

"Okay, Candance. Please! I get it."

I sat down on the bed and had to come to grips with myself. My mind was wandering all over the place. I just couldn't believe Mark showed up. This was by far the craziest thing he'd ever done. My head was reeling and spinning. I had to think things through for a moment. I knew I had to talk to him. He crossed the line completely. He was acting like a psycho!

Ignoring my girl's reactions, I immediately grabbed my cell phone next to the bed. I needed to give Mark a piece of my mind. This trip was supposed to be about me and my girlfriends. His ass was always in desperate need of my attention. After turning my phone on, all at once, it flooded with messages. Again, my mind was blown by Mark's behavior, and I just couldn't process what was happening. I needed to take a breath and relax for a minute.

"Lisa, are you okay?" Lauren interrupted. "Because you look like you saw a damn ghost!"

I was in complete shock.

"HELLO?" Candance shouted and snapped her fingers in my face.

"Are you ok?" Justine said, cradling me. "Is everything okay?" she persisted.

"You guys, I'm okay. I just can't believe Mark's psycho behavior."

"We told you that fool is crazy."

"Candance, please!"

"I'm serious Lisa. This is a damn red flag. He has some attachment, abandonment, and stalker issues. This is on a whole new level. I'm talking about some investigation discovery bullshit. Girl if I were you, I would…"

"CANDANCE, PLEASE!" I shouted. "You know what, I'll deal with Mark later. I'm not about to let his ass ruin my trip. Let's just go back to bed. We're seeing Kendrick Lamar tonight and we need our rest." No one said a word, and they all agreed.

It was around 7:30 in the evening when we left for the concert. We were laughing and smiling on the way down to the lobby. We were going to dance and party like we were twenty-one. But as soon as we stepped out of the elevator, there was Mark. I couldn't believe my eyes. He had been sitting in the lobby the entire time with a sad puppy dog look upon his face. I told my girls that I would catch up with them later. The looks on their faces were completely priceless.

I immediately approached Mark sitting in a lounge chair next to the elevator. He was looking down at his phone and appeared to be texting somebody. Walking towards him, I could feel my veins pulsing in my neck and held my clutch so tightly. I felt as though I was going to rip it in half. I walked hard in my black heels, and the sound of the stem echoed on the marble surface. "What the hell are you still doing here?" I said, towering over him.

"Baby, please listen to me. I love and miss you. I just wanted to surprise you and I…"

"BOY, SHUT YOUR WHINY ASS UP!"

"Lisa, you're making a scene," he said, getting up. He grabbed me by the arm while dragging his luggage in tow with the other. "Security is going to put us out of here. Can we just go to your room and talk?"

"Mark, take your ass home! I don't have time for this bullshit. I can't believe you showed up here. This is by far the most outrageous, psycho, and craziest thing you've ever done. I gotta go…"

"Baby, please! It's really important."

He continued dragging me towards the elevator.

"MARK!"

"Lisa, stop yelling."

He pressed the third floor, and the elevator doors opened, and we argued all the way to the room. People were staring at us. I was so mad at Mark. He kept on persisting that he missed and needed to see me. He claimed it wasn't his intention to ruin my girls' trip. He felt that he didn't do anything wrong. "MARK, PLEASE LET GO OF ME!" I yelled and tried to force my hand out of his grip. Then, with his other hand, he took my clutch and took my key card out.

"BOY, YOUR ASS HAS DEFINIETLY LOST YOUR MIND!"

"Lisa, please!"

He aggressively pulled me into the hotel room. He threw me on the bed and as I tried to get up, he climbed on top of me. He started kissing me down my neck, towards the valley of my cleavage, and aggressively on the lips. His kisses muffled my moans. I was beginning to give in by the seconds. He slowly began caressing my tights and down my legs. My hands wrapped around his neck, and I gave in to his demands completely.

Day 3. Around 2 a.m. I awoke to the sound of Mark snoring and could hear someone talking in the adjoining room. The door was closed, and it sounded like Candance was talking. I made out a little of what was being said. They all agreed they were done with me. After hearing this, I got up, put on my robe, and knocked on the adjoining door. Surprisingly, Mark was still sound asleep.

As I continued to knock, no one opened the door. "I can hear yall." They didn't say anything else, and I saw the lights go out from underneath the door. "Please! I'm sorry you guys. Please! Open the door. I'm sorry." They didn't respond. I knew the next day things were going to be awkward. I stopped knocking and sat on the floor in front of the adjoining door. I was contemplating everything that had happened. I had betrayed my girls. I didn't know how I was going to fix things and gain their trust. So, I got back in bed and decided to sleep on it.

Mark and I didn't wake up until about 11:30 a.m., and I could hear someone knocking at the door. I immediately got up, grabbed my robe, and let the housekeeper know we didn't want service. When I turned around, Mark was up, and I could see the look of satisfaction on his face. He was smiling boyishly and was propped up on his elbow. Then, he lowered the sheet down to his waist. So, I could see his abs that were firm and glistening from the sun shining through the windows.

"Baby, why don't you come back to bed and let me take your worries away? You look stress boo."

"Mark, I can't. My girls are pissed at me. I have to fix things and you need to leave."

"What? It's like that?"

"No, Mark." I sat down on the edge of the bed, with my arms folded, biting my lower lip.

"Baby, your girls are just jealous of us."

"Hardly, if anything? They think you're a psycho, and they're trying to save my ass!"

"That's because they don't know what real love is. Anyways, I don't want to talk about them. Let's just get a shower, breakfast, and I promise I'll be on my way. Plus, I heard your girls leaving their room about an hour ago. Honestly, I don't think they're worried about you."

"What they left an hour ago?" I got up and started pacing back and forth.

"Yes, that's what I'm saying. They were making a lot of noise and talking shit about us."

"Mark!"

"I'm serious boo! Let's just enjoy the rest of the trip together."

I couldn't believe they just left without even talking to me. I quickly grabbed my cell phone out of my clutch.

"Boo."

"Shut up, Mark!" I called all their phones one by one, and it went straight to voicemail. I even tried texting, and they didn't respond. I had blown it big time. I knew it was going to take a miracle to fix things. I was mad at myself and thought about all the times I managed to ruin our get-togethers. Eventually, I stopped trying to call and text my girls. I plopped down on the bed, and Mark sat up and tried to comfort me. He could see the tears welling up in my eyes.

"Baby, it's going to be okay."

"SHUT UP! THIS IS ALL YOUR FAULT."

"MY FAULT."

"YES, IF YOUR NEEDY ASS HADN'T SHOWN UP!"

"MY. NEEDY. ASS."

"YES."

"Ok, let's stop yelling," he calmly retorted.

"I'm not yelling."

"Anyways, your girls are gone. Let's get a shower and we will discuss this over breakfast."

***

Day 7. My girls were really done with my ass. I didn't manage to get in contact with any of them. They had switched hotel rooms, changed their itinerary and flight. Now I knew it was going to take a lifetime to fix things.

Mark didn't make things any better. When he found out that my girls ditched me, he ended up staying. We didn't have a good time either. I kept on thinking about hanging out with Candance, Lauren, and Justine. I desperately wanted to make things right, but it would take some time and distance from Mark.

When we arrived home, Mark and I agreed to take some time apart. Now I could see what everyone had been talking about. I had decided to stay with my parents for a couple of weeks. My Mom was beyond ecstatic to have me in her company. With Mark out of the picture, we were able to make up for the lost time.

When I returned home, Mark and I argued a lot about the smallest things, from coffee to television. Some days we would bicker for hours. Eventually, I started sleeping in the guest room and couldn't tolerate him. Then, one day we decided to split. I had to be the bigger person and move out of my apartment.

As the months went by, Mark found another woman to stalk. Now that I was free, I spent enough time thinking about how badly I hurt my family and friends. I was so mad at myself for putting Mark on a pedestal. I tried to fix things with everyone, and they didn't want to have anything to do with me. Somehow, I was going to find a way to gain their trust, even if it was going to take a lifetime to salvage any relationship.

Not just A Friend

At first, I thought I was just a good friend. I'm that ride-or-die type of person when it comes to my friends. When they need something, I'm always right there on the double. They can call me whenever they need a favor, and I'll drop everything at a moment's notice! My friends know they can always count on me. They say, "I aim to please."

When Gina needed a babysitter, I was the first one she called. I was glad and pleased to do anything for her. There were no ands, ifs, or buts about it. I showed up and watched those cute little kids from sunup to sundown. While she was out, she didn't even bother to call. She knew her kids were safe with me.

And how about the time, Tasha needed a ride to work for a week. I'm the one who gladly volunteered to pick her up to and from work. She was so happy that I agreed to do it. Being the good friend that I am, I didn't even charge her gas.

Then, there was Tom, who needed to borrow a hundred dollars just to make ends meet. I proudly drove to the bank, withdrew my money, and handed him the cash without hesitation. There were no questions asked. The following week when Tom got paid, he didn't even pay me back.

My friends and I went out for drinks just last week and somehow, they forgot their wallets. So, guess who politely picked up the tab? I did. The next time we went out, they had forgotten their wallets again! Hey, I didn't even complain and picked up the tab again!

Then, this past summer, my girls and I took a road trip to Vegas. I had to be the one to drive us because everyone seemed to have issues with their cars. So, I politely drove us there and even filled up the tank. On the way back home, no one offered to drive or fill up the tank.

Now here I am, in desperate need of a favor, and no one comes to my rescue. My car has broken down, and I'm stranded on the side of the road. I've tried calling and texting Gina, and she didn't bother to pick up. I even told Tom it would cost me two hundred dollars to have my car towed and asked if he could loan me the money. He wouldn't even give it to me. Then, I tried reaching out to my girls, and they didn't want to have anything to do with me either. They all had some excuse about not having any gas or money. So, here I am, stranded in the middle of nowhere. I am contemplating all the nice favors I have done for my friends. Now that I am in trouble, I don't have a single friend to help me out.

Painful Management

Being a latch key kid has its perks since there is little or no adult supervision. You can do almost anything. I remember there were times when my parents were too busy working, and I'd be gone for days without them noticing.

My friends and I used to pile up in my ride and leave town. We'd all go from Hollywood to Vegas in the same week. We were driving around acting stupid, hitting up the local bars and nightclubs with our fake I. D's. If we flashed our money, no one seemed to care how old we looked. They were sure to let us in. Life was a gamble, and we stayed playing games.

Soon, we quickly became bored with running the streets. Our homes became the local hang-out spots for raiding the fridge, swimming, playing video games, and throwing parties. Man, life truly was fun! But soon enough, we got tired of just hanging out. It just wasn't exciting anymore.

So, we decided to turn things up a notch when I introduced everyone to my parent's mini bar. They had every type of liquor you can think of. So, we started with small sips, then moved onto shots, and graduated polishing off bottles.

While we kept hitting the sauce, we would dance, giggle and parade around until we got sick. Then, do it all over again the next day. I remembered drinking so much that I couldn't even go a day without a drink. I would start with a glass at breakfast and top a bottle off by dinner. I even drank so much; I even started carrying a flask. I would drink at school, work, and even drank while driving. Luckily, I didn't kill myself or anyone. I was fully functioning, and no one seemed to notice, not even my parents.

When drinking no longer gave my friends and I a buzz, we eventually moved on to the best next thing. We wanted to numb ourselves from ourselves. While no one was looking, we started raiding medicine cabinets. The side effects from the pills we popped began to numb our pain. We were addicted to the feeling of going in and out of consciousness. We didn't have to feel or think about anything.

So, yes, being a latch key kid has its perks. When no one is looking, you can almost get into anything. Sometimes you lose your way, and sometimes, you find your way back. So here I am. "Hello, everyone. My name is John and I'm an addict."

Generation X vs. the New Millennium

"Our generation used to believe in doing something. These new millenniums are changing our way of life."

"What do you mean?"

"Well, back in my day, we believed in going outside. I remember we used to play from sunup to sundown. Every kid in the neighborhood used to come outside and play. We'd jump rope, played hide, and seek, freeze tag, and ding-dong ditch. Nowadays, I don't see kids playing outside anymore. Your generation has changed today's youth."

"We do hangout!"

"Yeah, that's the thing. For you, hanging out is sitting around, watching YouTube videos, listening to music, looking at gadgets and having coffee in the middle of the day."

"Well, that's what's we like to do."

"Nah, looking at the internet all day, shouldn't be the thing to do. You should be outside enjoying the outdoors. Walking, running, hiking, and throwing a frisbee or something."

"Ha...ha.! Your funny Uncle. I'm too old to be throwing a frisbee."

"Girl, your age has nothing to do with exercising."

"Your generation is lazy and don't want to do anything but stay plugged in. How is that any fun?"

"Well, it's not that we're lazy. It's what's in. We like to stay connected with one another."

"Meeting people! Now that's another thing. How do you meet someone online? When you don't even know who you're really talking to?"

"Uncle, it's called facetiming."

"But, who's to say their telling the truth?"

"Uncle Charlie, people will lie right to your face."

"Well, that's true. But when I was your age, we believed in meeting people in person. We'd sit down and talk to each other face to face. We called it socializing and it had nothing to do with the internet. Social media has killed the old way of communicating. I don't know about you Renee, but I prefer to meet people in person."

"I know Uncle, but that's the old way of doing things. Our generation like to scope people out. See what they're into. We like to look at each other pictures, post, and see whose following who."

"Ha...ha...I called that stalking."

"I don't."

"I just think your generation is out of tuned with the real world. Yall, stay connected to your phones, tablets, and laptops. I remember my friends couldn't wait until the weekend and hangout at the mall."

"Personally, I like taking my phone everywhere I go. It's my lifeline. It's how I keep up with everyone. This way, I don't miss out on anything. As for the mall, its dead Uncle Charlie. Nobody shops at the mall anymore. You can buy everything online."

"Ha...ha...if you say so. Yall, new millenniums are really starting something with all that online shopping. You heard of the retail apocalypse?"

"Yes! And it doesn't have anything to do with online shopping for the most part. It's the economy. So, people are spending less on material things. Anyways online shopping is just so much easier. You don't even have to leave the house or get out of bed."

"That's laziness."

"No, it's efficient."

"Yes, maybe. But I love going shopping. You can see what you're really buying. But that's not my point. When you get out and go places, you meet people."

"Well, not anymore. You can meet people online. It's fun, quick, and easy. There's no awkwardness."

"Awkwardness? I call that breaking the ice. See your generation don't know how important it is to socialize. Verbally communicating is one of the most important things you'll learn in life."

"Whether you talk online, or meet in person, I still say your socializing?"

"Ha...ha....your funny."

"Laugh all you want. Meeting people online is the new way of doing things. Hell, almost everything!"

"I know and I find that very sad."

"What's so sad about it?"

"Well, nowadays technology seems to prevent people from interacting with one another. When you walk down the street, people don't even say hi anymore. They're too busy looking at their phones. I even seen people almost get hit by cars while crossing the street because they're trying to text. It's just sad."

"I'd have to agree with you on that one. It's not that our generation doesn't like to communicate in person. Nowadays, it's all about convenience. It's just, the way of life now. Technology is taking over. You can now check yourself out at the grocery store, don't have to drive, or park your own car. You see Uncle, it's not that our generation don't believe in doing anything. Technology has just consumed every aspect of our lives and sometimes there's no way around it."

"I know. Isn't that something?"

"Yes, because if you don't obtain a skill that involves using your hands, or doing something that a computer can't do, you're basically shit out of luck."

"That's why it's important that your generation, the new millennium get out there and start doing things. Otherwise, the future is going to be one that's unfulfilling."

"Easier said, than done. Especially, when technology makes everything so much easier, faster, and quicker."

"See your generation is entertaining the idea of being more convenient."

"I must disagree with you Uncle. What can you do when the world is changing all around you?"

"That's a good question."

"You're either going to remain the same, or either move along with it. So, you see Uncle, it's not about going back to the old way of things. It's all about adjusting and finding a way to fit in. I know it sounds like a tragedy, but if the world is changing, you may have to change right along with it."

"You're right. I guess I didn't see it that way. I'm just sadden by the way the world works today. People are no longer communicating face to face. Technology is taking over. I really don't know what to say about our future."

The Hoodie

I never thought I'd catch so much slack for wearing a piece
of clothing that keeps me warm, comfortable, and sleek. I love
my hoodie and like to tug upon its sleeves. I love to pull the
hood over my head. Somehow, I feel safe and shielded from
the world. So, why is that such a bad thing? I just don't

understand why so many people are threatened by this article of clothing. I can't believe the world is telling me I shouldn't wear a hoodie.

I used to remember the days when clothing was an expression of oneself. People used to admire one's style of clothing. They used to say, "I love that shirt, or where did you get those shoes?" Nowadays, you don't want to be caught with the wrong shit on. You might lose your life over it. I just don't know when the world started making a fuss over one's clothing. I thought one was entitled to free will. Now fashion has become a dangerous thing-a single threat.

So, I'm going to decide to take matters into my own hands. I say, "Hello world, who are you to judge?" Oh, you think I look like a wolf in sheep's clothing! Well, I beg to differ. I'm going to wear what I think suits me best.

Handcuffs! They say I fit the description of a suspect! They think I'm a threat! A danger to society for the simple fact that I'm wearing a hoodie.

Excerpt from Dark *Nature Uprising*

Coming soon Fall 2027

In 2045 the earth was nearly destroyed by the accumulation of pollution in the atmosphere. Humanity was quickly becoming extinct, and we were running out of time. Food and water quickly became scarce, and life became unsustainable.

Luckily, NeuroCorp. Industries, a titan bioengineering company I worked for developed a new controversial electro photosynthesis beam. This device could replenish earth's natural resources. Never had it been imagined that our planet could recover from certain doom. Life on earth had become far- reaching with exponential growth. Resources were abundant. Humanity returned and vowed to protect our newfound salvation.

When all seemed quite right in the world, scientists at NeuroCorp quickly discovered this newfound technology could do so much more. Not only could it enhance our planet, but it could alter and change human life itself. One day twelve of us researchers were invited to witness this life-altering event. But little did we know, we were the experiment.

I remember that day clearly. We all were excited to be the first to witness something that could alter human life. But as soon as we reached the lab's basement, they locked us up one by one in empty padded cells and exposed us to an extreme dose of the electro photosynthesis beam. Some of us could withstand the intensity of the energy surging through our bodies, while others were reduced to ash in a blinding pulse.

The exposures had different side effects on all of us. Before the exposure, I was nearsighted, short, skinny, and physically weak. Now I am 6 foot 2, muscular, and strong. My arms, legs, and abdomen were perfectly crafted and toned. I had biceps that were full, firm, tight, and glistened as my veins reigned through them like intricate lines on a road map. My vision also became clearer, sharper, and stronger. I could see farther than the human eye could see. I also could see through any object and right down to the details of its genetic makeup. I also had the ability to focus my thoughts to a degree of telekinesis and move objects with my mind. My abilities were my secret to escaping the compound. Others weren't so lucky and became permanent residents of NeuroCorp. They were now held captive and became weapons of mass destruction.

***

It has been several months since I escaped from NeuroCorp. I had spent most of my days hiding out in a forest near Los Angeles, regrouping, researching, and retracing every inch of my plan to infiltrate NeuroCorp. Due to my enhanced abilities, I had a photographic memory of the exact blueprint and location of the bio electro photosynthesis beam.

I stood out in the distance on a roof top overlooking the facility. I could see NeuroCorp. and how it stood out like a beacon amongst the rest of the buildings in the heart of downtown L.A. These buildings all looked old, abandoned, and were surrounded by shipment containers that were brought in by the nearby ports. However, NeuroCorp. was the only industrial building that was fortified by an electrically charged rampart and an intriguingly solo female guard.

In a matter of moments, this was all going to change. As I climbed down the rooftop stairs and headed to my car, l thought about my mission once again. I would pose as one of the scientists. Then, sweet talk the brown-eyed woman at the main gate, set chargers and take out a couple of the parked tanker trucks, wait for everyone to come running out, make a run for the metal doors, head for the elevators on the northside, descend to the lab, and destroy the array.

I slowly drove my recently acquired black Navigator through the white barricades in a slow zig-zag fashion. I quickly adjusted the collar around my white lab coat once more, grabbed my makeshift badge, and slowly came to halt by the armed guard. She cautiously proceeded to the driver's side, and I let the window down.

"I.D. and nature of business?" she said firmly.

I quickly handed her my I.D, and she looked at me with intensity. Her light brown beautiful eyes zoomed in on me as if she could see into my soul. I tried to give her my best award-winning smile. Her full pouty lips didn't wince, flinch, or move an inch. The longer she stared into my eyes, the more I began to feel very strange. There was something vaguely familiar about her.

"What's the nature of your business sir?"

"I'm Dr. Braverman and I'm a genetic physicist at NeuroCorp."

"How come I've never seen you before?"

"Because you were blinded by these guns," I said, making my muscles flex underneath the white lab coat. The female guard looked a bit taken back, and I could see her beautiful lips beginning to form into a smile. Her stance started to become a little more relaxed. *I knew it; these guns get the ladies every time.*

"Excuse...me?" she hesitantly replied.

"Ah, there it is. She smiles and it's even more beautiful than I could ever imagine." She flashes another broad smile, and her eyes become a little more gentle and softer.

"Sir?"

I started batting my lashes as she was drinking me in and started gazing at the dimple in my chin. "Yes, beautiful," I softly murmured and locked eyes with hers. Now I could remember why she seemed so familiar. She was one of the twelve. Her, name was Haley and she used to be an intern at NeuroCorp. The longer we looked into each other eyes, the more connected we felt. I could sense the energy surging inside of her. She was trying to pry through my inner thoughts, but I was able to shield them with false memories of us working together. Then, she started to ease up a little and gave a slight smirk. Now I see why NeuroCorp. only had one guard at the gate. Haley was one of their weapons, a construct of an innocent human-like illusion but a threat underneath it all.

"Dr. Braverman, is...it? Have we met before?"

"Yes, in heaven."

She started laughing and smiling.

"Please, I'm serious," she laughed.

"Aren't you an Angel? I think I'd know an Angel if I saw one. You truly are heavenly with those beautiful brown eyes, high cheek bones, luscious locks, and gorgeous smile." Her face was starting to light up. I had her all riled up and could feel her energy surging throughout her veins. She could no longer handle the emotion that was bottling up inside of her. She quickly handed me back my Id and let me pass through the main gate.

I quickly found an emptied parking spot and grabbed my duffle bag loaded with hell's fury. I set the charges around several nearby tankers. They were all rigged for ten seconds. I slowly counted, "five...four... three... two... one." A loud earth-shattering explosion rang out, and the ground shook beneath me, knocking me off my feet. I quickly got up and saw hues of orange and yellow glowing in the night sky. Then, I ran back to my car and crouched down, and stuffed the remaining chargers inside a briefcase.

Amidst the chaos and commotion, they were flooding out of NeuroCorp. I could hear alarms blaring and security teams briefing to lock down the building; only seconds remained. So, I decided to make a run to the metal doors. I remained unnoticed as I quickly ran in while others reeled past me.

After several minutes, I eventually made it to the end of the corridor with no problem, but I saw a tall, white, bulky man heading straight for me when I arrived at the north elevators. He was dressed in all black, medium build, and appeared to be security.

"Sir, where do you think you're going? All personnel are to evacuate immediately."

"I'm...Dr. Braverman. .. I need to get to the lab and secure my research specimens."

"No one is going anywhere, but through those doors," he sharply replied while pointing towards the corridor doors behind me. "And how come I've never seen you before?"

"I've been working here for years. So, could you please move out of the way? It is very important that I secure my specimens." The security guard eyed me once more and stood in an aggressive stance. Then, he grabbed my right arm and threw my briefcase onto the ground and pinned my arm behind my back.

"Buddy, you're not going anywhere," he growled.

I quickly tripped him with my leg and spent him around to the ground. Then, he grabbed me by the collar, rolled me over, and landed on top of me. He tried to punch me in the face, but my enhanced reflexes stopped him. I was able to grab his fist midflight and held onto it tightly. He tried to free his hand from my grip, but I was too strong and crushed the bones in his hand. He immediately loosened his grip and rolled off me and looked down at his hand. He tried to let out a scream, but the pain was too intense. He was trying to catch his breath as he belted out,

"HELP!... AHH.SOMEBODY HELP!" he cried out in agony.

I quickly ran towards the elevator and hit the button. Just as the doors opened, staff came running out, almost trampling me. I eventually made it inside and could still see the security guard flailing like a beast on the floor. The doors shut, and I hit the button for the basement. Automatically, a virtual keypad appeared. *Oh...no... I need a passcode to get into the basement.* I started pacing back and forth. *I can do this.!* So, I started to calm myself down quickly. I stared at the keep pad and tried to concentrate. The numbers quickly began to form in my mind. *5, 13, 27, 62, and 15.* I immediately punched the numbers in on the virtual keypad. The elevator started making its way down to the basement. Then, the elevator came to a halt and the doors opened. Suddenly, I was overwhelmed by a strong intensity of light. It was so bright that I couldn't see beyond it. I felt the intensity of it radiating through my body as my back was pinned against the elevator wall. My body began to shutter, and feelings of vertigo set in. Something was pushing against me. I couldn't keep my eyes open, and all went dark.

ACKNOWLEDGEMENTS

Thank you to my family and friends who always believed in my passion and joy for writing. Thanks for letting me spend countless hours bothering and interrupting you about sharing my stories. You were my true motivation to putting these words to paper. Although I'm a small voice in this world, sharing my stories with you is more significant than anything.

Thanks to all the people who gave me a moment of their time. Your generosity and kindness go a long way. Being able to share my passion with you is truly rewarding.

And a special thanks to the future generation of this world. These stories belong to you and the everyday struggles you may face in finding your way. Sometimes we rise, and sometimes we fall. But at the end of the day, you can always get back up and start over again.

Thank you.

When Mrs. April L. Engels does not have her head in a book. You can usually find her enjoying the great outdoors in California, fishing, hiking, gardening, and spending a day at the park with her loving daughter and husband. Also check out her other great reads *Whimsical and Fanciful Women* a collection of young adult short stories about the desperate lives of women and her children's book *Playtime* on Amazon. Look out for her new upcoming book *Provoked* Summer 2026.

To The Reader

It is truly rewarding to share my passion for telling stories! I love bringing joy into people lives through literature. Reading is especially important and without your contribution, the life cycle of a book cannot be complete. As a part of that process, reviews are critical to the life of books. If you could be ever so kind to leave a review on any platform where your favorite books are sold. One comment goes a long way. Thanks for your support and please continue to share the joy of books!

Thank you!